BORDERS

Published & Unpublished Articles Only

Md Anowar Islam

ISBN 978-93-5458-071-0

Published in India 2021 by Pencil

A brand of
One Point Six Technologies Pvt. Ltd.
123, Building J2, Shram Seva Premises,
Wadala Truck Terminal, Wadala (E)
Mumbai 400037, Maharashtra, INDIA
E connect@thepencilapp.com
W www.thepencilapp.com

Author biography

ABOUT THE AUTHOR IN BRIEF

Born of a middle class family, the author, Md. Anowar Islam is a lawyer and journalist by profession and passed his Matriculate examination from S. Ali Govt. Aided High School, Sukchar (Assam) in 1977 and completed his Arts Graduation from Tura Govt. College (Meghalaya) in 1981. He pursued his higher studies in law in J.B. Law College, Guwahati and obtained LL.B degree from there subsequently and completed Master Degree in Arts from Gauhati University thereafter in 1990. He also passed the NCTVT training course in stenography from Tura ITI, Tura earlier. He entered government service early in 1981 and served various departments both under State mad Central Governments at Guwahati, Goalpara and Tura. He also served as Lecturer in Goalpara Law College for sometime, as also in Kazi & Zaman College, New Bhaitbari and then in Hatsingimari College. He joined the Tura Bar Association sometime in 1992. His journalistic works started practically as back as in 1979 immediately after successfully participating in the Competition Success Review Essay Contest No.293 and has by now composed a large number of poems in English, Assamese, Bengalee and Hindi as well. He has also established a good rapport as an outstanding educationist, author, writer of note books and poet and has had a lot of published works done and contributed to different dailies of the North Eastern Region and joined as an active mofussil newspaper reporter sometime in 1991 and associated himself with The Assam Tribune, The North-East Times, The Meghalaya Guardian, The Shillong Times and as a freelancer to The Telegraphs etc. and so on so forth. His poetic compositions have come to be published in different local books and magazines while his efforts to publish a local BI-lingual weekly, Sapta-Dhwani from Hatsingimari (Assam) from February, 2000 as the founder editor, although could not be successfully carried through, yet brought him acclamation from all corners. He has associated with different social organizations and served as Members and Advisers in different organizations like the Meghalaya Board of Wakfs, Assam Unnati Sabha, Animal Welfare Board of India, Total Literacy Campaign, West Garo Hills district, Meghalaya, Founder President of Hatsingimari Press Club and so on. He has also been honoured with Rashtriya Rattan Award in 2004 , followed by an Award given away by a Dhubri-based local weekly publications group. He has been a great social activist rendering social services all through his life in association with Red-Cross Society and many other local NGOs and will continue to serve the people as such in all future to come. At present he is practicing as an Advocate under Hatsingimari Bar Association, and holding a key position of Headman in his own eleca with sufficient pull over the mass people.

-------Author.

CONTENTS

Foreword

Forward

This book is a collection of all the publisheshed and unpublishd articles I subscribed or contributed to different newspapers of North East Region of India during early years of my life. The articles were relevant at that time and some of the might carry relevance even to this day as well. I am sure the articles and more particularly the tititle of the book on which man to man division is sought to be created or maintained by our people throughout this region or even throughout India or even the globe today, may be chrished by the esteem readers if taken in in their right perspectives. However, I being a journalist by profession as well as as a lawyer, tried my level nest to ensure that not much sensitivity is created by my articles, nor any major mistakes orrors are left out in them. And if the esteemed readers find any fault or error here or there, I shall be highly grateful to them if they could point out the same and give proper suggestions to improve the sthe next editions. I thank the Pencil management to have provided with the opportunity to go for sel-publication of this book through its forum. I also thank the Executive Manager of Penvil Management, Ms Gargi Madam for guiding me all through the publication works done by me herewith. With these few words, I thank one and all once again. ---Author

Preface

Preface

I am a lawyer and journalist by profession. My career started as a Stenographer in Posts & Telegraphs Department sometime around 1981. Before this, as a student of Pre-University in 1977-79, I started writing in news papers and magazines in a smaller scale, and won a Commendation Prize & Certificate for successful partivipation in an Essay Contest in 1979 written on the subject - India of My Dreams. Thereafter I graduated myself as an Arts Graduate in 1981 from Tura Govt College and joined the Central Govt.job as mentioned above almost simultaneously selected through SSC Examination. I comlleted my law graduation degree in 1989 and Master degree in Arts (English) in 1990. I joined as a Lectuerer in Goalpara Law College, then as a Lecturer in Kazi & Zaman College, New Bhaitbari as well as at Hatsingimari College one after another. I started law practice in 1992 at Tura Court under Tura Bar Association and practiced law in Meghalaya High Court for sometime as well. Now I am practicing as a lawyer under Hatsingimari Bar Association duly registered as a member of Bar Council of Assam etc. I was the founder President of Hatsingimari Press Club and Member of Animal Welfare Board of India, Hatsingimari Unit, Member of

Assam Unnati Sabha, Hatsingimari Unit, Member of Literacy Mission, West Garo Hills, Tura and Member of Meghalaya Wakf Board as well. I had also clise association with Red-Cross of India and different other NGOs and Mahila Samitis, educational institutions and their managements too. Presently, I am running 3 schools from primary, upper primary upto secondary/higher secondary level duly sponsored by Down-Hill Minority Education Trust at Hallidayganj, West Garo Hills, Meghalaya. I have been a great social actist and so honoured with Rashtriya Rattan Award in 2004 and an Award given away by a local newspapers group at Dhubri (Assam). I am committed t dedicate my my life towards the cause of huminity during the rest of my life.

Chapters

Introduction

On Geographical Borders

It is indeed a fact that the problems of different geographical borders have come to divide people from people spliting their hearts into two halves from time immemorial. History has never remained static and with the passage of times it has continued to change demography of different countries, their system of administration, their borders and so on. An effort has therefore been made to remind ourselves as to how cruelly time has changed our minds, sense of belongingness, attachment and detachment to one or the other society, states and nation and what not. We live together showing ourselves to belong to one nation and yet divide ourselves in the name of caste, creed, community and religion and create artificial barriers between two people and feel graced or disgraced in gaining or losing something out of such barrier that form the basis of future geographical borders.
The international border between India and Bangladesh or any other nation, the inter-state border between Assam

and Meghalaya or other states, the inter-district or inter-subdivision borders or boundaries that have come to be carved out by people at one point of time in the past as
1 advantageous for themselves have come to be the cause of disadvantages for the people of the present generation. Similarly, those which are being carved out today as advantageous for ourselves are not unlikely to be the cause of disadvantage for the next generation, and the process goes on. And yet we cry hoarse as to what he or she has got and what I have not and the crisis lingers on unmitigatingly. The division of India into India and Pakistan on communal line has borne its brunt. So has the division of Pakistan into Bangladesh and Pakistan. The division of Assam into several smaller states has also not quenched our thirst for dividing our people in the name of caste, creed and community etc. All these divisions have but divided our people with their heart divided into two halves. Half of the heart living in one country or state or district or subdivision while the other half living in other ones, and thereby we have not gained anything but lost many things. The most precious thing that we lost is the Peace of Mind. I have seen people living in India with their kith and kin living in Bangladesh to cry in silence. So have I seen people living in Meghalaya with kinsmen living in Assam die in utter desperation or frustration and often creating sort of problems about their being branded as outsiders or foreigners within their own motherland and what not. All these are but the bitter reward of divisions of people and creation of barriers by
2 different man-made borders and boundaries only. If this becomes the fashion of our day that one demands for something and he quickly gets it too, there is no point

then to deny the same thing of the same kind to another, as it creates sense of suspicions, and ultimate alienation. The disuniformity that has come to be maintained in the name of development of one with constitutional safeguards provided thereto, has indeed been viewed with suspicions by many and it has got to be remedied sooner or later in order to allay the fearpsychosis of the so-called disaffluent section of the people facing virtually ban on all fronts at all times starting from settlement unto survival with dignity. The question of being a Hindu or a Muslim, a tribal or a non-tribal is nothing but creation of times. No one is a Hindu or a Muslim, a tribal or a non-tribal. It is all the creation of ours. We are above all human beings and let us survive together with harmony and endeavour for equal march and development. Because, we are all but different parts of a single body and the body cannot be healthy if all the parts are not equally taken care of. So is the case with our nation, states, districts or subdivisions which must not be sidelined in dividing or subdividing them all and more so in the race of obtaining powers and powers only. Let us put our heads together and see for ourselves as to why we cannot march ahead without dividing our people and their hearts into two halves, and ensure that discrimination is not made on consideration of 3 caste, creed, race, community and religion anymore in our country for an equal and concerte development of our people. And yet in case, we need to go on dividing ourselves, let us not divide us in a way which ultimately needs to be repaired and remedied by the future generation without first putting in a similar strenuous effort and toilsome pains to get back to its original shape for no fault

of them.
-----Author.

o0o

4
Chapter-II World

World Peace and the Future of Human Race

Science of mankind is replete with a host of human concomitants. Peace is an indispensable concomitants to human beings. Human races without peace is deplete while peace is defunct without human existence. A life with fear of attack or that of an imminent extinction is no better than a deceased. The future of human race and whether or not it is on the verge of extinction depends much on the point of world peace. Human survival, therefore, calls for an unperturbed peace of mind, body and soul as well.
It is noteworthy that the fear-psychosis of Soviet subjugation developed out of the World War II led to a steep race on nuclear proliferation. Nuclear testings began to be carried out in an unabated rate. Both America and Russia emerged the two Super Powers in the field. It continued uncountered and has now taken therefore the form of a menace leading the world to a nuclear holocaust. The US commitment to continue with its Star War programme has again poised a renewed threat to the world peace and human existence. This
may, in all ugliness, lead Russia to start a like
5 programme who are temporarily at a relaxed option

now towards nuclear arms race. It is, therefore , not beyond anybody's guess as to what may happen with the fate of human race and the earth if by any accident or mistake Star War takes place.

Today the world stands at the most crucial juncture of what may be termed as Nuclear Era. Almost all the developing and under-developed countries of the world still depend much on the aids and assistance of either of the two Super Powers. And it has been the folly of the Super Powers to fondle with the weak nations over the years only to fulfil their set policies and purposes. The American double standard has again been the hardcore force creating from behind the scene more global problems. Attempts are very often made to set one nation on the other with the objet to subverse and subjugate them. The increasing trend of terrorism, internal coup and clashes, guerilla warfare etc. are some of the results of such subversive interference only. This will be manifest from the recent American bombing in Libya, their subtle help to Pretoria regime in South Africa, their shameless interference with Grenada, Nicaragua and the like. In addition, war between non-aligned nations like Iran-Iraq in the Middle East, nuclear mishaps like the Chernobyl, growth of more advanced technology etc. have worsened more and vitiated the climate of peace and human survival to a great extent.

6 The concept of disarmament and nonalignment developed at a time when the world faced with an increasing trend of nuclear race. Most of the peace-loving nations like India missed not, after all, to realize the gravity and dimension of the devastating menace poising on earth by this race. This undesirable race of nuclear arsenal has

been resented strongly from various corners of the globe. The non-aligned nations in consonance with the Third World countries also urged the Super powers for limiting the race. They have very often been taking to c criticize and condemn their nuclear policies to uphold the cause of human survival and world peace. But all such gesture of criticism, condemnation and persuasion failed to bring about any progress towards disarmament trailing many more hot events.

What can be concluded from the above is that the natural tendency of human decay is indispensable. History witnessed at certain intervals of time, such decays of human race by way of war and pestilence. The same tendency is perhaps going to repeat only through a nuclear war for supremacy. Auttohan, the inventor of atom bomb, is perhaps distressed weeping today in the Heaven and Einstein, maybe, got crying blind to see the incriminatingly evil consequences of what they brought out and left behind to prove to be useful to the mankind. The times is ripe now we realized the gravity of nuclear aftermath and take to work for peace and harmony. It invariably calls for a
7 strong Consensus and singleness of mind to avoid hostility and confrontation.

The sense of unanimity must grow in everyone to bring the people at large under a single umbrella of a war-free universe. This is yet another aspect, which needs a meaningful thrust to be given first. One must wonder that in the name of advancement we are pushing ourselves into the knawing jaw of the secret machination of a giant like science and technology. Let us not use them for destructive purposes. Let us, therefore, work for stopping

this devastating race in order to ensure world peace and future human survival, which appears to be quite unlikely to remain as peaceful and undisturbed as desired by the world community under the given circumstances.
(Filed to the Essay Contest organized by Lachit Rovers Crew, Bharat Scouts & Guides, Guwahati, Assam by A. Islam as a participant to the Contest during 1985-86)

o0o

8
Chapter-III India

India of My Dreams

When we hear of the word - India, we very proudly proclaim, " India is our motherland and it is a Sovereign Democratic Republic state". NO doubt, India is a democratic state and is independent of any external interference. She has gained her independence on August 15,1947.
So far as the British history as well as the history of the world is concerned, once, " The sun in the British Imperialism did never set". The English, who dominated colonialism all over Asia, Europe and Africa, subjugated India also. But now India is no longer under foreign rule. It is an independent state and has its own government. It is also a secular state. India is no more a backward but a underdeveloped country. She has brought about an all round development in countrymen's lives.

In terms of economic strength and national integrity, the Planning Commission of India has undoubtedly made an immense progress towards agro-industrial development. But food production in India has not proportionately been increased to feed the unusually increased number of its population. From this standpoint, India's proclamation to be self-sufficient is not true. The
9 overall food problem could not fully be mitigated.

The recent drought all over India has indispensably proved government's inability to face and solve such natural calamities. The drought has alarmingly caused great harm to paddy and jute plantation. Several innocent lives also have been lost and succumbed to death due to acute water-scarcity and excessive heat especially in Bizarre. So, this year paddy growth seems not to be upto the mark. It indicates India's bad and inauspicious future.

Apart from all social, scientific and economic achievements successfully made, India's present internal position is not orderly and smooth. Since Janata party came into power in Centre as well as in various state assemblies, there have been prolonged and never-ending controversial disagreements prevailing among the party leaders. Different coalition governments in different state cabinets having no stability have become subject to President's rule and re-elections. Due to such repeated dissolution of state cabinets and lack of smoother administration several mob-violence and communal riots etc. have come into operation in various states and union territories like Mizoram with great rapidity and acceleration.

Moreover, there are political parties, whose main objective is to bring a crack in Janata Party, committing mischief but

trying to impose upon government's shoulder. They are hoarding
10 indirectly and smuggling the essential commodities resulting in an unusual price rise. Such mischievous and disastrous activities and occurrence of riots etc have brought countrywide sufferings and terrorism in public lives and in future these will bear nothing but destruction. Unless government have a prompt visualization on these undesirable happenings, such unsympathetic tragedies will bring forth nation-wide disintegration and devastation. Famine and starvation will soon take place. No welfare will be achieved. Chaos and confusion will spread far and wide resulting in inability of progressive performances on government's part. Our country will lag behind and shall remain ever backward and undeveloped.

(After Matriculation, contributed to Essay Contest No.293, Competition Success Review, New Delhi, Results declared adjudging the participants Competition Success Stars, awarding High Commendation Merit Certificate to the winner, A.
Islam, among others-1979-80)

o0o

11

Need for Re- Emancipation of India

The dastardly act of assassinating former Prime Minister and Congress (I) President, Rajiv Gandhi by bomb blast at Sreperumudur near Madras on May 21 last has dealt a very severe blow to the World's largest democracy of India. It is a great tragedy for the bereaved family, a national crisis for India and an irreparable loss and insurmountable setback for the party and its millions o supporters, especially when election process to the 10th Lok Sabha and almost all the State Assemblies were still midway.

But then it is also a colossal loss for the countrymen at large. In fact, the whole world was dumb-struck at the premature end of this leader, who rose to the stature of a world statesman within a short span of his political career with potential promises for future generations forever.

There is no doubt that Indian people have enough strength and courage to forebear such national crises. But yet apprehension looms large as to a grave threat to the democracy and secularism in India. Although the remaining two phases of elections are being held under tight security arrangement, political leaders of all shades are today far more apprehensive because who knows who makes a murderous attempt when and on whom. What ails one most at the present critical 12 juncture is how the coming days, months and/or years are likely to pass with India's decades-long democracy and secularism because violence or terrorism in India is now almost a regular feature and has surpassed all proportions, for which the politicians themselves are squarely responsible. Because their involvement in increasingly corrupt

Practices, no-secular behaviors and indifferent attitude towards common wellbeing have all rendered India economically far weak and indebted to foreign bodies and so forth, giving way to all sort of internal troubles.

The aftermath of Rajiv Gandhi's assassination, which took tens of innocent lives in different parts of the country, is yet another instance of barbaric intolerance and wrathful frenzy prompted by the ideas of vengeance or reprisal, when none could yet wipe out the unpleasant memory of genocide that followed Indira Gandhi's assassination seven years back in Delhi.

Atop all these, there is the unabated acts of caste and communal violence, killings here and killings there of innocent people by so-called terrorist outfits and groups.

Not a single day passes today in India without claiming innocent lives through ruthless killings by this or that extremist groups. Where do all these lead us ?

Assassination of Rajiv Gandhi during his election campaign equally gives vent to great many questions. Who was/were the actual culprit (s) behind this barbaric assassination ? What might be

13 the real motive behind eliminating Rajiv Gandhi ? And so on. Without however any prejudice to the probe being conducted into the case presently both by an Inquiry Commission and an SIT(CBI) separately, the second question may lead us to somewhat a clear-cut conclusion – termination of dynastic rule in India, although involvement of foreign power seeking India's destability or that of some terrorist outfits for their own causes may not also be ruled out altogether. As to the first question, however, the assassin's identity by and large being still unknown, any premature comment may prove but misleading and far from being warranted.

Now that the Gandhis, I mean those capable of claiming immediate legacy, have been eliminated, the era of dynastic rule is, temporarily, if not permanently, over in India. Because the question whether Sonia Gandhi or for that matter Priyanka Gandhi will be willing to fill the vacuum created by Rajiv Gandhi's elimination is still a matter of conjecture only. This thus renders Congress (I) party virtually without any shade of Nehru-Gandhi family for the first time ever since our Independent existence.

It is now only that the acid test whether Congress (I) can survive with equal dignity, respect and pull over Indian people as before, starts and the result will be seen within the next few months or years. However, it is no denying the fact that Rajiv Gandhi's brutal assassination has placed Congress

(I) in a most dwindling position which may

14 ultimately prove quite detrimental and fatal to its very unity and existence as one of the oldest and most influential national parties in Indian political scene.

There are various considerations which but impel one to draw such a foregone conclusion as below:-

Firstly, so long Congress (I) was considered as the largest single national party reflecting the wills and fulfilling the aspirations of Indians right from the Freedom Struggle, as it was adored by a long panel of virtuous leaders. The Gandhis, although had some shortfalls, were not totally devoid of such virtues. But the rest that fill Congress (I) rank and file now are by and large opportunists and susceptible to transfer loyalties. Absence of a truly virtuous and strong leadership has thus brought Congress (I) down to the level of all other national parties, which are but frail and weak in terms of organizational set-up, stronger leadership, useful outputs and so on.

Secondly, the leadership crisis, which gripped the party following Rajiv Gandhi's assassination and could somehow be overcome by choosing unanimously Shri P.V. Narashima Rao as its President, is not unlikely to emerge and shadow it once again in the probable ride for Prime

Ministership amongst the party stalwarts in case it secures majority Lok Sabha seats.

Should such a race start in Congress (I) rank and file, this single largest national party may split
15 once more incapacitating itself to provide any stable government at all. In other words, the party will lose its pan-India character and their government, if formed at all, relegate itself to face equal fate as did the Morarji Desai Government in late seventies and the V.P.Singh or the Chandra Shekhar governments in the last Lok Sabha.

No such apprehension, however, will be there if it fails to win majority seats to form Government at the Centre, although uncontrollable lust for power may induce a section thereof to break-away nevertheless and form splinter parties too. But then dangers to India's democracy and secularism will still lurk loose because of lack of a viable and strong alternative leadership to run a democratically established and relatively stable government at the Centre.

In this context, the following lines from an article (The Sunday Times, London) authored by Tony Allen Mills and reproduced in the North East Times on June 7 last may be cited:

"Dynastic politics have endured in India only because so few credible alternatives have emerged from the ranks of the opposition. Those non-Gandhis who have assumed supreme power in Delhi have
generally made a mess of it."

From the above remarks and that o the below–quoted lines from another article published in the same newspapers, the position as to how far the other parties (Congress-I not included) can

15

provide stability and save India from probable onroads on its democracy and secularism may well be assessed:

"………How it is, when India's main political parties are faction-ridden, corrupt outfits most of them are, where caste consciousness shadows almost every encounter between ordinary Indians, where the country is so vast, various and
violent, that the nation holds together? "

Although the writer, David Selbume, attributed the answer to the above question to "India's black polity" -- a corrupt system very much functional in India – and said that patronage, bribery, sycophancy and obedience help hold up the pillars of the Indian State, Parliamentarism etc., he missed not to see the hold unfastening gradually too.

He want still a step further to term Congress
(I) party as "Policyless" requiring a strong leader which they do not have at the moment, and said separately:

"….. In today's India, politicians
must match cunning with cunning, and violence with violence; compared with it, the Raj was a golden era."

He also expressed apprehension on firmer maintainability of secularism vis-à-vis the growing impact of the Hindu fundamentalist BJP, whose future growth, though may be checked by sympathy for Rajiv Gandhi temporarily, is certain to create mass clashes between the Hindus and the Muslims

16

---- the two major communities in India. Secularism, which he termed as the fragile plant in India, is squarely threatened at the instance of VHP, which vowed to raise 1 million volunteers to demolish 3000 mosques in the country. Where lie then the democracy, stability and the hard-maintained secularism in India ?

In fine, we, the Indians, stand right now at the crossroad of highest order of civilization and meanest form of barbarism side by side unwitnessed in the entire history of civilized survival of mankind. It needs us to look back and ponder a little while because our beloved motherland is crying for our unfettered help once again to re-emancipate her now from the shackles of overgrowing terrorism, caste and communal violence with potential threat to democracy and secularism and so on.

(Filed to newspapers on June 8, 1991 by A. Islam)

o0o

17
Need to curtail Electoral Rights in India

The constitutional provisions as regards qualification etc. for a person being chosen a member of either House of Parliament or State Legislatures have been enumerated under Article 84,102,173 and 191 supplemented by those of the Representation of People's Act 1951 Accordingly, for being chosen as such member, a person should, inter-alia, be a citizen of India and not less than 25 years of age, in case of Lower Houses and 30 years of age for Upper Houses of Parliament or State Legislatures, as the case my be, besides being an elector of a parliamentary or assembly constituency in the state or union territory concerned.

There is no bar of educational qualification, nor to simultaneous nomination of a person from more than one constituency, nor even to re-election of such member with any prescribed age limit, both upper and lower, as is normally enforced in case of government employees including high court and supreme court judges.

Article 326 of the Constitution supplemented by relevant sections of the Representation of People's Act, 1950 & 1951 again provide for election on the basis of Adult Suffrage. Accordingly, a citizen of India completing 21 (now 18) years of age is entitled to vote in an election.
18
No other qualification is prescribed either of sex property, taxation or perhaps of education etc., although persons otherwise disqualified under law on grounds on non-residence, lunacy, crime, corrupt or illegal practices, are debarred from exercising the right.
The populist slogan of electoral reforms, raised initially under the aegis of Jan Sangha, a party, right back in 1968 is yet to achieve its real goal. Admittedly, reduction of voting age down to 18 years and enactment of Anti-Defection laws are the two bold but not at all foolproof steps towards this end of Rajiv Government during late eighties. The euphoria of these reforms perhaps withered away soon after because of various reasons. The proposal of further electoral reforms which has had a long halt once again with the fall of NF Government are, undoubtedly, ideal enough but how long to wait for their practicalisation?
India today lacks in that very value-based politics which she had about 40 years back or so. It has turned into profession, rather lucrative profession and hence one is seen involved in active politics interestingly even till days

before retiring for eternal abode or so.

The behaviors of present-day politicians with too many obsessions to the idea of electoral abuses arisen out of a strong desire to stick to this lucrative profession, and that of the electorate in terms of voting pattern having been plagued by mass
illiteracy or ignorance, has only vitiated
19
India's political atmosphere to an almost unimaginably irretrievable depth. These intriguing impulses, corroding all democratic values have undergone, save deterioration, no perceptible change over the years. Our politicians, who even the AntiDefection laws also failed to prevent from resorting to frequent political hegemony, are perhaps too conscious to be moved by any such phenomenal degeneration. Contrarily, many of them, who are simply self-centered, complacent and desperately power-hungry, are averse to any change and do wish the situation to linger on to their political advantages. So is perhaps the case with the mass electorate, who tend to remain ever ignorant and superstition-bound despite changing scenario all around them and the globe.

The progress prosperity, security, integrity and sovereignty of the nation depend much on the personality, honesty, talent and knowledge
(including conscientious election by the electorates) of our political representatives. When such politicians or such electorate, as are invested with enormous electoral right, themselves lack in proper education, there is always a possible mess being created by them in the respective domains. Such a mess has already been created several times in the past giving way to instability, wastage of time,

energy and scarce national resources. The messcreating syndrome becomes far more pronounced when the illiterate electorate fails to vote for a right person or at best choose an illiterate or under-

20

educated person unable even to understand the basic implication of legislation, far less to take an active part in the deliberation of the House.

The mushroom growth of illiterate or undereducated politicians, as also the illiterate electorate with extreme electoral flexibility is, thus, a menace and has virtually led to a steep competition in political arena and further degeneration of voting pattern. Regionalism, which is now far assertive in all parts of the country, including election of frequent hung Parliament or Assemblies, is but the unpleasant outcome of such competition or degeneration only.

Moreover, lowering of voting age down to 18 years, at a time when 70 percent of our people do not really understand the meaning of democracy and are inclined to harp on extra-emotional ideas due to illiteracy and ignorance and plead that cheating of a candidate once money is received in promised exchange of vote is a sin likely to affect their children" health might have also added to the aggravation.

The voting age was lowered perhaps on wrong logic, first of a person's having acquired, at the age, necessary eligibility for a government job, including defense services; secondly, because a person o the age becomes, under law, major or mature for all practical purposes. Apart from the fact that age alone cannot make a man eligible or a govt. job, the arguments put forward on majority grounds that

different legal statues treat the issue(s)
21
differently only to conclusively confirm that age, majority and maturity may not run concurrently.

In this context, according to Order 32 of Civil Procedure Code, a "minor" means a person, who has not attained majority (i.e. 18 years of age which is 21 years in case of a minor under a lawful guardian or the court of wards (S.3 of Indian Majority Act, 1875). The majority criteria for a female and a male for marriage is 18 and 21 years of age respectively—a female and a male being minor and incapable of giving consent. But under Sec. 83 IPC, a minor above 7 but below 12 years of age is liable for committing crime, if he attained sufficient maturity of understanding. If not, it means, is not liable.

The rule under Sec.82 IPC, by which an infant below 7 years of age cannot commit a crime, because of insufficient intelligence for the act, has perhaps no analogy in the law of evidence since such an infant, under Sec. 118 of Indian Evidence Act, is competent to testify as a witness provided he understands questions and gives rational answers to them. Thus, understanding is the sole test of competency bearing the impression of maturity in legal matters concerned evidences. Hence, there seems to be no uniformity of laws regarding maturity or majority of a person.

Right to vote, which is incidentally a most significant constitutional right and does not tend to be valued equally by an illiterate and a literate
22
persons alike, obviously for lack of adequate intelligence of the illiterates, should not have been conferred to all on

mere analogy of age. Ironically this is being done in India. The fact that one has to attain certain age is undeniably a precondition and implies attainment of majority or maturity to become a voter. But can age alone be the final test of majority or maturity?

The question of equating an educated official of defense personnel with an illiterate person based mainly on age and an assumed maturity o understanding but not on any other consideration, say, o education, for their practical adaptability, and conferring thereupon the right to vote to them can well be compared with "feeding the baby with an indigestible only when it needs simple cow-milk" for survival and growth. The result of such thoughtless act is obvious dyspepsiac fermentation and consequent instability of body, mind and soul….!

Age, therefore, can in no case is the final test of majority or maturity; nor be there any golden yardstick to measure it except that we adopt it on rational basis to suit our purposes best. The question of imposing some other pre-condition should accordingly find primacy in order to leave no room for unconscientious casting of votes. What might have been the role played by our illiterate voters in the past or at least in the two preceding general elections held in 1989 and 1991, when there emerged but hung Parliament and hung Assemblies

23

most? The answer is not that of easy-going riddle. But what wrong it is to try out?

It is a fact that more than 50 percent voters participated in every post-Independence election. This is, undoubtedly, a positive sign of attainment of maturity by them. However, how far the illiterate electorates are or were conscious or how enthusiastically or unenthusiastically do or did they come out to vote is still a mysterious question virtually knowing no answer. Had there been no overactive or anti-social elements influencing through muscle or money powers or masterminding these voters to their own advantages and not otherwise, the percentage of votes so cast would have gone far down. Admittedly, it politically educates the people, but should it confine within collection of votes alone?

Meantime, terrorism, which is yet another weaponry to dictate terms, has raised its ugly heads now in interfering with election process as well. It has got its impact on the electorate too. It may be noted that India witnessed the bloodiest of elections this time with record number of loss of human lives including that of Rajiv Gandhi under election-related cast and communal violence, terrorism and so on. None can perhaps imagine that elections had to be counter-manded in so my constituencies and reelections ordered to staggeringly higher number of poll booths following killing of candidates, rigging, booth capturing and violence. One can

24

scarcely think of a free and fair poll in our country, if this trend continues to prevail in the days to come as well.

What is more appalling is that even the national party politicians, who think at least twice before irritating their party high commands, are also not inconspicuous by any measure in directly or indirectly involving themselves in mischievous acts despite party ideologies. Many such parties again hesitate not even to harp on non-secular propagation, including violence, rigging, booth capturing during elections at the cost of all virtues and pressing national needs and interests.

The need of the hour, therefore, is more of curtailing the right to vote and to be voted with reasonable restrictions imposed upon illiterate citizens for which amendment to the Constitution and the Representation of People's Act may have to be considered with due earnestness.

Accordingly, among others, acquisition of a minimum of educational qualification, say, HSLC, may be made one of the preconditions for a citizen for entitlement to right to franchise. Also adequate thought be given to adoption of two different majority criteria, say, 18 years for the duly qualified or educated and 25 years or more for the illiterate citizens, for conferring right to vote. Also sufficient economic back up including giving a days' w ages to each voter for casting vote on poll day may be considered by the government.

Similarly, a minimum education or

25

qualification, say, HSSLC for membership of state legislatures and graduation for that of Central Legislature may be fixed. In addition, it should be made a convention to allow persons having a good and clean social background only to file nomination for elections. The amount of election security is raised to a still higher sum. None should be allowed to seek reelection for more than two terms with rigid limitation of upper age for retirement or so. Also the practice of seeking election simultaneously from two or more constituencies be disbanded. Pension benefits to legislators should be given only when one retires from politics.

The measures, besides reducing the scope o steep competition in politics and its sad fall outs manifested in the shape of violence rigging, intimidation etc. will act as a great disincentive to all and sundry including non-serious candidates making bids for such membership. Meanwhile, the measures suggested on conferring right to vote including giving wages to voters is expected to ensure conscientious election of our political representatives besides discouraging application of money and muscle powers etc. in election.

(Published in The North East Times, Guwahati dated September 2, 1991 By A. Islam)

o0o

26
Waning Profile of Leadership Genius

A glance on the current political scenario of India pinpoints to a very fast waning profile of leadership genius and lack of a righteous leadership to guide the nation in right direction.

As a matter of fact, there has occurred an "unprecedented dearth" of a true leadership genius whose political thought and action, sense of social responsibility, moral stand and philosophy, if any at all, can be termed as constructive, honest, sincere and rational in character, spirit, inspiration and essence.

This, by far, is indicate of an extreme retardedness of our people hindering growth of our people and development in all spheres of life, though there had certainly been no dearth of learned men, more concerned with religious injunctions and teachings than about modern, scientific and basic or higher education in medieval India at par the West.

By modern, scientific and higher education, I mean university education, which is considered to be the surging fountain producing a true leadership genius.

It may be recalled that even during the initial stages o its introduction a great majority of the Indian masses had openly and desperately discarded English of western pattern of education, which they considered to have had the ultimate goal

27

of imposing western culture on them at the detriment of their own.

Only a microscopic section of the Indian having embraced English education as the "gateway to intellectual flourishment", people could progress very little in this regard and had, as borne out by history, remained pleased with becoming what is called a mere clerk and other subordinate officials to the British Raj.

In the woods of an eminent personality, as also a contemporary freedom fighter of India,

Sachchidanda Sinha, "Our universities have rendered.... Great services to India. Assuming the correctness of..... Our critics..... that our educational system was originally designed to produce mere clerks and subordinate officials..... it has long since belied the intentions .... By producing not only almost all our great leaders but also those who have been successful workers in various spheres of public activities .... Which has ushered in what is popularly known as the great Indian Renaissance." It is, therefore, far more evident that once on the wake of English system of education becoming increasingly popular amongst the Indian masses, amidst subtle opposition from the orthodox section, India acquired the minimum leadership elements with a true nationalist philosophy, idea, spirit and inspiration, rabidly acceptable to the masses, the very dearth of leadership genius disappeared

28 gradually leader her to the path of a broad-based freedom movement.

The hard and strenuous efforts put in and immense sufferings undergone our past leaders are unparalleled for whose generous sacrifices again we could enjoy our hard-fetched Independence and are proud of it today.

Meanwhile, with the presence of those great souls around us, the very dearth of leadership genius had never again been sensed until such time as late Srimati Indira Gandhi was, on October 30, 1984 brutally assassinated by none other than her own securitymen themselves, leaving too large a vacuum to be refilled in any near visible future.

Here again, I may quote from an article of the noted journalist, M.V. Kamath, " Mahatma Gandhi created some leaders, Jawaharlal Nehru ignored it, Indira Gandhi destroyed it", and say that the leaders India produced under the direct inspiration of Gandhiji and like others did shed like the old tree leaves one by one in their natural course of life or fell victims of the unfortunate power-games India plunged into after achieving freedom.

It is interesting to see why leaders like Sri Ramakrishna Hegde, Sri V.P. Singh or Sri N. T. Rama Rao should not find national prominence and recognition to be capable of leading the nation in right direction vis-à-vis Rajiv Gandhi, till the other day a pilot only, whose knowledge and wisdom in politics seem to be as good as that o a man riding a horse without adequate knowledge how to ride it, 29

and yet managing the Prime Minister's affairs, no matter with what degree of perfectness and political maturity.

Unfortunately, however, the manner in which today's political leaders, inside and outside the Government, are engaged in deviating from moral virtues, democratic principles, national ideas and set public goals, the country can expect nothing concrete of such complacent leaderships, whose prime concern has become amassing wealth and gripping powers only. In any case, there seems to be no rescue from these complexities unless the sols of our leaders are purified through right education, right training and spiritual uplift. Hence unprecedented it is, and the state of affairs which India is passing through today in terms of leadership crisis is but unfortunate and has remained no longer a euphoria to any citizen of the country.

While speaking about education and training, I once again venture to quote the first Indian governor-general of free India, late Sri C.

Rajagopalachari : " To manage the affairs of an independent State, trained leadership is necessary….. University education is nothing but a training for leadership".

This in itself bears testimony as to how much stress and importance was put on education and leadership training while to quote Mahatma Gandhi,

"I will have our leaders teach us to be morally supreme in

the world", one wishes that this

30

very moral aspect was not lost sight of under any circumstances.

In fact, almost all of our past leaders had all the virtues --- moral, intellectual, spiritual and so on --- blended in them who received their education and political training both within the country and abroad. They had the requisite wisdom and vision to be guided in their actions by the principles of morality, devotion and dedicatedness. They had received their moral training and learnt to respect others' sentiments under the direct and pioneering inspirations o our various leaders like Gandhiji and others, and reached public heights thorough hard and strenuous endeavors.

Moreover, they had in their mind an active instinct of self-introspection so as to rise above the prejudices of all-personal gratification and selfaggrandizement at the expenses of national interest.

Here once more to qoute from Sachchidananda

Sinha, "If you indulge in introspection --- as I trust you do --- you must have realized that your fallings are mainly due to the facet that though you intellectually assent to many things, your feelings and emotions stand in the way of your carrying them out in practice." I wonder whether our present leaders do think seriously on the line of selfintrospection.

It is a common parlance talk that "before poking nose on others' business, oil your own machine or set your own house right first."

31

Leaders of yesteryears did always resort to constructive

criticism provided there was sufficient ground without harbouring on undue and false propaganda, which might mislead the people, and more so, unless they were pretty sure of no selfdeficiency and self-demerits, which might stain their character, integrity and personality with indelible black spots.

However, the practices of most present politicians unwarrantedly scathing and criticizing one another, feeding the citizens with deliberate misinformation, exploiting public sentiments and rousing communal passions including undermining the democracy and democratic institutions, as also pointed out by our President, Sri R. Venkataraman, in his last Independence Day address to the nation are far more damaging and dangerous

It does not behove to a morally upgraded and honest leader of true nationalistic spirit and inspiration as well, which stand to reason as to why India lacks in a dedicated leadership, whose moral stand, personal integrity and sense of sacrifices for the cause of the nation and its people can be put, beyond doubt, to test and scrutiny.

No doubt, not all of our past leaders were free from perverse idea and attitude in their thought and actions. To quote Sachchidananda Sinha still once again, "It is a matter of common experience in this country to find people, in all spheres of life, professing views and sentiments which they not unoften act".

32

However, inspire of such perverse aspects that found place in their minds, some of them had displayed their right sincerity, honesty and maturity in doing the right job in right time so that nobody could question their integrity and purpose of action.

While alluding to the honesty, sincerity and maturity of our past leaders, I am not inclined, however, to say that our present leaders are all insincere, dishonest and immature not capable of doing any right job at all. No doubt, more universities have come up in our country over the years, and the number of educated and highly qualified citizens has also gone up substantially. What is, however, actually perturbing is that the leaders produced by these universities are far more perverse and evasive in their idea, attitude, thought and action.

The present politicians do not seem to have received the right education and right leadership training, or could in them be inculcated the spirit of nationalism, dedicatedness and moral responsibility towards the country and the citizens. Most of them are also spiritually much more retarded and are either handicapped in right earnest to appreciate the need of the hour or are less interested in looking into the life of those seventy to eighty percent of the citizens living in villages.

In any case, they have not undergone the odds of the nightmares of freedom struggle suffered by our past leaders nor have they put in any hard labours in becoming leaders. In most

33

cases, either they hail from highly placed families having no touch with the suffering lots, or the offshoots of unemployment problems and such other vagaries of life devoid of any leadership qualities, wisdom or vision, most prone to personal prejudices, self-gratification and so forth. Hence, they can hardly realize the agony of sufferers, not to speak of respecting sentiments of the suffering lots. Mahatma Gandhi said, "We can not be wise, temperate and furious in a moment". In fact, our present leaders are neither wise, temperate nor furious but are the mix of all the three. Nobody can at the same time be a critic, fan and admirer of a person, and do give an honest service to the nation and its people. Unfortunately, our most present politicians are the sumtotal of all the three necessary evils.

The spectre of corruption and complacency including the characterstic defects of our leaders poising too much wise and too much stupid simultaneously only to be swept away by the greed of powers and lust for wealth have take so deep a root, far more virulent in form, which unless rid off soon and the waning profile of leadership genius thereby reversed is likely most to cause an immense and irreparable damage to the nation.

(Published in The Assam Tribune, Sunday Reading, dated October 2, 1988 By A. Islam)

o0o

34

Development of the office of Governors in India

The office of he Governor was created first by the Royal Charter of 1600, which authorized the East India Company to elect a Governor annually to run the administration of the Company government in India, and the Governor carried on his administration initially with the assistance of Deputy Governor and the Court of Directors. The Charter of 1661 further authorized the British East India Company to appoint Governors to administer the territories in India under its control. Thus, the three Presidencies of Bengal, Bombay and Madras were placed each under a Governor for administrative convenience. Accordingly, the office of the Governor stands to be the oldest office in India's administrative history. Meanwhile, in the context of introduction of the authority of Parliament in British India following abortive consequences of the Dyarchy earlier introduced in Bengal, a new office of the governorgeneral along with four Councilors, was created under the Regulating Act of 1773 for the administration of Calcutta Presidency. He was again also given the power of superintending and controlling the administration of Bombay and Madras Presidencies respectively. The Governor-general was also authorized to

appoint Lt. Governors in 1835 subject to

35

approval of the Crown, for administration of different Provinces, as also, in 1854, to appoint Chief Commissioner or an office to administer any territory under his control with the sanction of the Court of Directors and Board of Control, later of the Secretary of State for India.

Meanwhile, the Governors of the Presidencies having been selected from the British public life, the Governors of Provinces, the Lt. Governors, and the Chief Commissioners were selected from amongst the ICS officers, who had served at least ten years in India. They held office for a term of five years and extendably could continue until their successors took over. IN addition to the extendibility of their term, they were also eligible for re-employment and cold is transferred from place to place. They could resign their office in writing. As regards their salary, it varies from time to time but the Legislative Council/Assembly had no power to vary their salary. The Governor could be suspended, removed and sent back to England by the governor-general and could be tried in a court of law for disobedience or failure to carry out any of his orders.

However, the Governor enjoyed certain immunities and was not answerable to any court for the exercise and performance of his powers and duties. Proceedings could be drawn against him subject only to two months' prior notice and no process for his arrest etc. could be instituted during the term o his office in any court.

36

The Governors, as the direct Agent of the Crown, occupied a higher status than the Lt. Governors and the Chief Commissioners. The Governor was an extra-ordinary member of the governor-general's Council should it hold its meetings within his jurisdiction, and could act as Governor General in leave vacancy. In fact, his role as the direct Agent of the Crown was of great significance.

Only the Governors could communicate direct with the Secretary of State for India. In the cases of Lt. Governors and he Chief Commissioners, however, the Governor General very frequently interfered with their functions, and had no power to correspond direct with the Secretary of State for India. Thus, the Governorship was considered to be the most complete form of local government with certain degree of independence, though the other two exercised only limited powers delegated by the Governor General.

However, apart from the Lt. Governors and t he Chief Commissioners, the Governors also were not absolutely independent of he Governor General's overall control and had to, to some extent, comply with his directions given from time to time. This is because the Governor General was the key-person and was responsible for the entire administration of British India. Though there was a division of powers and functions between the Central and Provincial Governments, the former always laid down the broad guidelines to be followed by the

37

latter. The Governors including the Lt. Governors and the Chief Commissioners were required to communicate their proceedings to the Governor General who maintained a close watch through its officers sent as to whether the subjects entrusted to the Provincial Governments were properly carried out or not.

The Government of India Act, 1915 provided that the Lt. Governors and the Chief Commissioners might or might not have an executive council. This was, however, totally negatived by the Act of 1919. But the Governor was invariably assisted by a legislative council, an executive council before the introduction of dyarchy and by council of ministers under the Govt of India Act, 1919 and 1935 respectively.

Accordingly, the Governor, the Lt. Governor and the Chief Commissioners were the Chairman/President of the respective executive council/council of ministers. But the Governor was not bound to accept the advice of his ministers. The Governor had to act on the advice of his ministers unless he saw sufficient reasons to dissent from their opinion. Thus, he was not a constitutional ruler, and had powers to override the Council of Ministers, and continued to occupy a dominant position even under the Act of 1935.

However, the Government of India Act 1919 provided that the Chairman designated as President, are elected by the legislative council itself from amongst its members, though the Governors

38 happened to be the President in the initial stages. Meanwhile, the person elected as the President had to be confirmed by the Governor. In the Act it was also laid down that the Governor should appoint the first President. The Governor had the powers to remove the President. The Govt. of India Act, 1935, however, did away with the practice of the President being appointed by the Governor. Since the introduction of Diarchy in 1921, the Governor could select the ministers who commanded the confidence of the House. From 1937 onward, however, the Governor has been empowered to appoint the leader of the party commanding absolute majority in the House as the Chief Minister/Prime Minister, and other Ministers only on the advice of the Chief Minister. He had some discretion in the selection of Chief Minister when no party was in absolute majority. The ministers, appointed by the Governor, held office during the pleasure of the Governor. He could appoint any person as minister who is not a member o the legislature subject to his becoming the members within a period of six months from the date of his being appointed as the minister.

The Governor had, thus, at all times, powers to appoint the minister, distribute portfolios and dismiss them also under Act, 1919. The Act of 1935, however, did away with the power of distribution of portfolios of the Governor, and instead it was entrusted upon the Chief Minister. Again, under Act of 1919 the Governor could take

39
over the administration of transferred subjects but the Act of 1935 vested this power with the Chief
Minister.

The Act of 1935 also provided for promotion of Joint Responsibility by the Governor not provided by the Act of 1919. The Instrument of Instructions issued to the Governor laid down that he should appoint his ministers who in his judgement was likely to command a stable majority in the legislature If the legislature expressed no confidence even in one minister, the whole ministry had to resign. In other words, all the ministers including the Chief Minister must sink or sail together.

Prior to 1921, the Governor, the Lt. Governor and the Chief Commissioner summoned, prorogued and dissolved the legislative council, and could extend the life of the council by one year. They had also the right to address the legislative council.

Moreover, no bill could be introduced in the legislative council without prior consent of the Governor. Every Bill passed by the legislature had to be presented to the Governor for his assent who might give his assent, withhold it or reserve the bill (including certain bills on specified subjects which he was bound to reserve) for the consideration of the Governor General under the Act of 1919 and 1935 respectively. Finally, all bills had to be introduced in the legislature with prior consent of the Governor.

The Governor had the power of certification
40 of the demands relating to the reserved subjects, rejected by the legislature, which upon such certification became law. Above all, the Governor had an extensive

power of rule-making for the conduct of the Government business unilaterally and legislative business in consultation with the Speaker. No Act made by the Governor could be questioned.

The Chief Commissioners, the Lt. Governors and the Governors had power to nominate certain number of members also to the legislative council, and the latter voted according to the directions received from the former. This was done by dint of his powers of nominating members, and the Governor carried on his administration practically with the help of the nominated members, whose number was as nearly as one third of the total strength of the legislature.

The Governor could recommend persons for appointment as judges o he High Court by the Crown. He could appoint any one of the judges of the High Court as acting Chief Justice and could appoint the Advocate General also in a temporary vacancy. He could grant reprieve to a person convicted of any offence against any law also.

The Governor was entrusted with certain special responsibilities under Act, 1919 and 1935 for protection of the minorities and backward tracts, maintenance of peace and tranquility, prevention of grave menace to the country, protection of the legitimate interests of the civil services, safeguard

41

the States' financial stability, combating terrorism and the like.

Moreover, besides exercising certain discretionary powers, the Governor was empowered to exercise some individual judgement powers, the former having been exercised without consulting the ministers, though the council of ministers had to be consulted by the Governor in the exercise of the latter without, however, any bindings to accept their advice.

As a consequence of the transfer of powers to the Indian hands in 1947, and the Constitution of India having been adopted in 1950, however, the powers and position of the Governors have undergone a radical change, which may require to be dealt with separately for convenient elaboration and fruitful comparative study.

o0o

42
Governors in Independent India

As against the pre-Independence colonial systems of administration, the Constitution of India provides for a federal Government, parliamentary in form both at the Centre and the States. Normally, it provides that there shall a President at the head of the Union Government, elected indirectly through an

Electoral College consisting of the members of both Houses of Parliament and the State Legislatures. The Constitution also provides for a Governor, appointed by the President and placed at the head of each State. The Governor holds office at the pleasure of and subject to removal by the President himself. The same person can be appointed Governor for two or more States simultaneously.

The President is also empowered to appoint Administrator, as his agent, with such designation as he might specify like the Lt. Governors and the Chief Commissioners for administration of minor States and Union Territories. In practice, however, it is the Prime Minister in consultation with the Home Minister only that makes the preliminary selection for appointing the Governors. In fact, before making appointment of a Governor, a tacit consent of the Chief Minister of the State concerned is also obtained.

The appointees for Governorships must be citizens of India above 35 years of age. They must

not be members of the State Legislature or the

43

Parliament. If such a member is appointed as Governor, he is deemed to have vacated his seat in the State Legislature or the Parliament from the date on which he enters the office of Governor. Finally, he cannot hold any office of profit. It may be expedient to mention that the Governor, before entering his office shall make and subscribe an oath to preserve, protect and defend the Constitution, as also to devote himself to the service and well-being of the people of the state concerned.

The Governors of major Indian States are selected from amongst the seasoned politicians, while those of minor States and Union Territories, i.e., Governors, Lt. Governors and Chief Commissioners, are selected from amongst the senior Civil Servants. However, the Governors in Independent India are not the agents of any authority, though the Governos, Lt. Governors and Chief Commissioners of Union Territories have to work as the agent of the President and independent of his Council of Ministers.

Incidentally, the Governors of the major States having

been selected mostly from the ruling party at the Centre, they tend, however, quite often than not to be the agent of the Centre and their office rendered, by dint of their frequent transfers and postings, to the seat of a musical chair game causing great harm to the sanctity of the institution.

This has, in fact, led to a severe criticism in different quarters, and the recent recommendations of the Sarkaria Commission, specially to the effect

44

that the appointee for Governorship must not be a politicians belonging to the ruling party at the Centre, among other things, thus, have unequivocally been hailed by all, which, if accepted and implemented by the government, is expected most to bring about still more radical changes in ensuring a strong and smooth State administration.

The term of office of the Governor is five years, but he can hold office until his successor takes over. It may be terminated earlier also by way of (I) dismissal by the President and (ii) resignation. There is no bar to a person being appointed Governor for more than once.

The Governor enjoys certain immunities, under Article 361 of the Constitution, which lays down that he shall not be answerable to any court for the exercise and performance of the powers and duties of his office. Further, no criminal/civil proceedings shall be instituted in any court, and no process for his arrest or imprisonment shall issue from any court during his tenure of office.

Meanwhile, the Governors, unlike the

Governors of the Presidencies, who were empowered to act as Governor General in leave vacancy during the

British rule in India, are no more entitled to act as the President or so, which only the Chief Justice of India is entitled to now. However, though not in diplomatic and military spheres, the present Governors are empowered to exercise powers analogous to those of the President
in the executive, legislative and judicial fields
45
respectively.

Again, even though the President exercises some control over the Governor through his powers of appointment and removal, it doe not seem that he will be entitled to exercise any effective control over the State Government against the wishes of the Chief Minister, who enjoys the confidence of the State Legislature. The President may, of course, keep himself informed of the affairs of the State through reports of the Governor, under Article 356 of the Constitution, which may lead even to the dismissal of the Ministry either. Nevertheless, the Governor is a constitutional ruler of the State without, however, any independence.

As against the previous practice of the
Governor having only a legislative council to assist him, the Constitution of India provides for a State Legislature consisting, besides the Governor himself, of two Houses in some States and one House in others known as Legislative Assembly and
Legislative council respectively. It also provides for an elected Speaker for the former and a Chairman for the latter. The Governor has, however, the power to appoint a proem Speaker/Chairman. Since the Speaker/Chairman is elected now, there is no question of confirming or

removing them by the Governor.

As regards ministry formation, there shall be Council of Ministers to aid and advice the Governor, who has complete discretion in the appointment of the Chief Minister. However, if 46 there is a party with an absolute majority and a recognized leader, the Governor has no discretion but to send for him. The Governor, however, appoints the other ministers only on the advice of the Chief Minister.

In fact, time and again, it has been observed that Governors, who are otherwise deemed to be the agent of the Centre, have to face yet frequent interference in discharging their functions, which are expected to cease only if the office of the Governor is filled up on the lines as recommended by the Sarkaria Commission.

The Governor is the executive head of the State. The Council of Ministers are collectively responsible to the State Legislature. The Chief Minister shall communicate all decisions of the Council of Ministers and furnish such information relating to the administration of the State and he may call for proposals for legislation to the Governor as. All the ministers shall hold office during the pleasure of the Governor, who can dismiss an individual minister at any time. His right to dismiss the Chief Minister, whose dismissal means the fall of the whole Ministry, is, however, subject to noconfidence to be expressed by the Legislature, except under a situation otherwise provided in the Constitution.

As was the practice during the British period, the Governors cannot distribute portfolios of the ministers. The Governor cannot take over any subject that my all vacant consequent on

47

resignation, removal or death of a minister. In such circumstances, the present practice is that the Chief Minister himself deals with and looks after these jobs. The Governor has the right to summon and prorogue both the Houses of the Legislature. He can dissolve the Legislative Assembly but not the Legislative Council, which is not subject to dissolution except that one-third of its members shall retire every two years. He can also send messages to and address the House or both the Houses of the Legislature also.

The Governor has also the powers to promulgate ordinances during the recess of the Legislature, but such an ordinance, when promulgated, needs to be passed by the Legislature within six weeks of its re-assembly. Otherwise, it shall cease to operate. Hence, his extra-ordinary powers of legislation stand substantially curtailed as compared to the British period. All bills should be presented to the Governor for his assent after passed by the State Legislature. He may withhold it or reserve the bill (including certain bills which the Governor is bound to reserve) for consideration of the President or return the bill to the Legislature. The Governor must give his assent to the bill returned to the Legislature but has been passed for a second time.

Thus, the Governor has also a suspense and pocket veto.

He has, however, no power of certification of
demands, as exercised by his British 48
predecessors. Further, though the money bills and such other bills connected with financial matters need to be recommended by the Governor, no other bill require his

previous approval before introduction in the Legislature. The Governor is responsible for placing the annual financial statement also before the House or both the Houses of the Legislature.

The Governors have powers to also appoint the Accountant General and members of State Public Service Commission, but has no power to appoint judges of the High Court except for recommending persons qualified for judgeship. He shares this power alongwith the Chief Justice of the High Court and the Chief Minister of the State concerned. As of earlier practices, the Governor has power to pardon criminals, grant reprieves, respites etc. to a person convicted of any offence against any law.

The Governor has also, besides the discretionary powers, some special responsibilities to be exercised with respect to development of certain specified areas, maintenance of law and order and economic advancement of certain sections of people.

The above discussions have, however, been made without touching certain aspects of less importance. This had to be done to concisely bring out some of the contrasting aspects of powers between the two Governors of pre and post

49

independence era.

To conclude, it may be noted that the growth and development of the office of the Governor is of great relevance and utmost significance. Inspite of various defects and other lacunae, which were apparently present in the powers and functions of the British Governor

General and the Provincial Governors etc., they yet appear to have, having undergone a radical change, formed the ultimate basis of the constitutional powers and functions of our present Governors and the President as well, who derive such powers from the Constitution of India and t heir consistency can perhaps be negated at no juncture of future course of administration in India.

o0o

50
On Eligibility of Governor in India

Article 155 of our Constitution provides that there shall be a Governor appointed by the President in each State who, under Article 157, shall be citizen of India, have completed the age of 35 years, and shall not be a member of either houses of Parliament or any of the State Legislatures nor shall he hold any office of profit.

It is, therefore, evident that the incumbent for Governorship need not necessarily be a seasoned politician, except that he is eminent in some walk of life and well acquainted with the constitutional implications of his duties and responsibilities. A smooth discharge of his functions will, however, depend most on his knowledge, experience and the overall efficiency he commands in administrative fields.

Meanwhile, the omission to specify in the Constitution in clear and unequivocal terms as to whether the incumbent for the institution shall be a politician or otherwise, seems to be a serious constitutional loopholes in maintaining its innate impartiality while dealing with a duly elected government and similar other matters.

This has, on the contrary, widened the scope of the Centre in monopolizing this institution and appointing governors from amongst the party

51

politicians, mainly in order to fulfil its whims and fancies through partiality, specially in the States where the government is run by some other party or a combination of such parties. Instances are replete as to how the Centre, by virtue of its being the sole sponsor for a Governor, intervenes frequently in his functioning, or of the Governor not acting in his fair discretion while dealing with certain subjects not specified in the Constitution or order to please his party high command. This is done, in fact, keeping in view his future prospects of being elevated to still higher rank or being brought back to active politics in some powerful position. After all, politics does have an intoxicating effect on a politician, which, once tasted, precludes acceptance of total hibernation.

The recent action of the Meghalaya Governor, Mr. Bhisma Narayan Singh, in so precipitously inviting the Congress (I) to form a minority ministry allowing more than necessary time for proving its strength in the face of strong counter-claims staked by the Opposition groups, is a clear act of bias in the handling of affairs and thereby permitting horsetrading, though not floor-crossing which is banned by the Anti-Defection law. Thus, it appears that the misuse of various discretionary powers vested in the Governor and mismanagement of the Raj Bhavan affairs has become prominent features and the order of the day.

Moreover, this pious institution seems to

52 have become more of a seat of Congress (I)'s musical chairs game and a means of providing partymen's loyalty than anything else which be noticed from the frequent transfers and postings of Governors from one place to another, as also in including them into ministerial berths, party positions and vice-versa.

In this context, it may be quite pertinent to quote Mr. Arjun Singh, a heavyweight for the Centre, being suddenly placed as the Governor of the Punjab for a brief period, who had in the meanwhile served the nation not only as the State Chief Minister earlier for two more terms but also as Union Minister for some time till his present assignment as Chief Minister, Madhya Pradesh. Who knows he will not be placed tomorrow as the Governor of Assume or Haryana to meet the party whims perhaps to dislodge the popular government there!

Considering such a poor shape of things in the world's largest democracy, where capitalizing all powers and monopolizing the constitutional institutions are the basic ideals and hardened practices of the Union Government, the Sarkaria Commission recommended and stipulated broad guidelines which, in the present context, may deserve special mention and unreserved appreciation.

According to the Commission's stipulation, a person to be appointed Governor, in addition to fulfilling the normal constitutional requirements,

53

should: (a) be eminent in some walk of life; (b) be a person from outside the State; (c) not be too intimately connected with the local politics of the State; and (d) be a person who has not taken too great a part in politics generally, and particularly in the recent past.

Further, the Commission has expressed, inter-alia, the desirability of not appointing any politician belonging to the political party at the Centre as Governor of a State where the government is run by a party other than their own, and suggested stopping the practice of a Governor, once laying down his office, returning to active partisan politics, perhaps keeping in view the musical chairs game of the Centre, and the like.

One recalls those pre-Independence days when Governors, acting as the direct agents of the Crown, were appointed mostly from amongst the Civil Servants in order not to leave any room for complacency and frequent intervention by the Governor General in a Governor's functioning. This had, in fact, kept away all political hegemony, and so far as our knowledge goes, could ensure a smooth, unbiased and effective administration in the State. I am pretty sure that these practices and conventions, the need for which has been realized by almost all of us, are in the offing, and are going to be revived and re-established on he lines stipulated by the Sarkaria Commission soon. Let us hope for the best and wish that good sense prevailed 54 on all at the helm of public affairs. We eagerly wait to see that the, alongwith the Centre, do with this particular piece of the Sarkaria's recommendation.

(By A. Islam, The Sentinel, dated February 24, 1988)

o0o

55

Marriage and Population Control in India

India, meassured by any yardstick, is an overpopulated under-developed country. Population explosion is higher here compared to many a rich and equally under-developed nations. She has to feed over 10 to 15 million new mouths each year, which is equivalent to that of the Kangaroo's. The projected population of India that may, by any account, reach by 2000 AD works out to around 1000 millions., which itself is indicative of a grave threat to the economic stability of the nation.

Hence, population control seems to have poised the prime concern for salvaging the country from the mouth of the gnawing giant of economic destability and other relative ills.

It is a pity that inspite of a steep rise in the budgetary allocations since Fifth Plan onward, and corresponding excess expenditures in sharp contrast with the various plan outlays our government could not hold and pull back the trend of population explosion and hence India's progress in Family Planning programme, launched early in 1951 still stands in a very poor shape.

We ah, however, no dearth of experiences that various vagaries --- social, religious, superstitious including mass ignorance --- have been the principal hindering factors slowing down

56 the progress of the onerous tasks undertaken in this regard by the government.

Nevertheless, one of the major causes of population explosion and tardy progress of its control is attributed to the early marriage systems still prevalent in some parts of our country. But one must agree also that our Government have not been successful in removing the misgivings people suffer from because of the indiscreet practices of jumping into some other fresher programmes without waiting even for completing the trial stages either of the one already taken up in hand.

Leaving aside the one already in hand well before examining its effectiveness or detecting defects, if any, and other shortcomings going wrong with the programme and remedying them accordingly appears to have become one of the hardened principles of various designated Government measures and policies. This is, more or less, evident from the advocacy of raising further the marriageable age while there are already the ones to prevent child/early marriages. This will, if taken, mean yet another trial of riding a new but equally lame horse only to pass on to catch hold of the third one, while the detecting process of he lameness or examining the overall viability of the second might still stand incomplete or even unexperimented in many respects.

As already alluded to, there are laws, which ban early marriages and the like. Despite such striding efforts various homogeneous social crimes

57

are still not on the wane, and flouting all legal and socio-religious barrages these are being frequently committed almost undeterred in different corners. However, aversion and lack of proper interests in tracing the actual defects and formulating necessary remedies thereof have let the doors of various such incriminating acts wide open leading to the so-called fresh and overriding legislations in no time, however, to prove equally unworthy and as ineffective as happened in respect of already existing legislations.

This has produced more sound than action like an empty

vessel sounding high and the real objective remaining ever unrealized, the nation is subjected to almost a daily-mooted legislation, unnecessary paper movements and wastage of both time and energy entailing more expenditure compared to the actual achievement.

In India, nearly 70% of the people live on traditional tillage; and almost an equal number o them still subsist under poverty line. Owing to the limited scope and being quite seasonal in their profession, most of the agriculturists and the labour forces have to whisk away much of their times idly. There is neither any provision nor any avenue worththe-name for their entertainment or merry-making. Naturally, woman becomes a very cheap and readily available source of their gossips, and the sole object of mer-making the pastime.

The chronic idleness of these people, low economic status, lack of proper education,

58 mushroom growth of hazardous slums in various cities, towns and other metropolis --- indicative of an uncivilized and indecent life --- are chiefly responsible for various sex-indulgences and consequent births, legitimate or illegitimate both at an unchecked and galloping rate.

Human soul is always inclined to enter the forbidden world. The more is the restriction, the more is the tendency to break it. Unlike the west, sex in India is completely a secret and sacred subject. Man and woman, under certain religious traits, are still not supposed to inter-mingle and mix-up freely together. Our social system also doe not allow it. Marriage is the simplest way to overcome this man-made barrier resulting in early marriages and other trailing problems.

Admittedly, inspite of enforcement of co-education, coservices and all such co-isms, the status of our women is still haplessly insignificant, while a man, having too much regard to his curiosity and cardinal desire, is simply discouraged from mixing up freely with his female counterpart. Instances are, therefore, replete as to many a youngmen going mad in illegal love-making and eloping with young girls and so on and so forth.

The exercises of prudish is yet another source of increasing enticement and added incitement towards solemnizing early marriages; while the system of polygamy, still in vogue mostly amongst the Muslims, is no less degenerating a factor further aggravating the situation.

59

Unfortunately, therefore, the result has been quite adverse to the nation commitment towards fighting the growing population menace, sometimes not even in tune with different customs and laws of the land either.

The mystics of s semi-nude woman, often depicted in different books, magazines and cinematography, is more apt to entice a man, while the same woman in complete nudity will generate abhorrence in heart and mind repelling public attention most. The curiosity to learn and enjoy such a mystery sustains till the full details comes out of it. So is perhaps the case with the mystery of sexual and physical relation of a man and a woman also which, having remained veiled, tends to create more heat than light terminating in a big zero result or instantaneous disenchantment, however, no sooner the mystery is unveiled.

Recently, I had been enjoying a strictly (A) marked picture in a Guwahati-based talkie. Every cine-goers' --- man and woman equally --- curiosity seemed ran enthusiastically high and higher gradually climaxing to have the first glimpses lest the opportunity should be missed. There was, however, a hasty exist after sometime of almost half of the spectators as the big cine don, Om Shiv Puri, on explaining some Indian sex problems, jumped into depicting various western woman characters in complete nudity; the glamour faded out and, after intermission, the hall was virtually deserted leaving inside a negligibly few sprinkled occupants only.

60

We have, therefore, seen that one is inclined, subject to the instincts of natural repulsion, to know and learn what once known or learnt is no more desired to be further known or learnt. Accordingly, there was perhaps no more to know or learn now about the film. They came, they saw, they got the point: as if their folly submerged, victorious they emerged! This is Indian psyche! Human desire has no end, yet, once tasted there is no more desire on anybody's part to have any more taste o a thing and that marriage is perhaps no exception to such an instinct leading, in most cases, to unhappy termination once the taste of sexual charm is over!

Needless to say, the principal grogramme devoid of any well-thought-out supportive measure is most likely to face with multi-dimensional challenges and eventually fall through. As such formulation of certain measures like Radio, TV and Video programmes in various regional languages, instead of Hindi ones alone, comprehended best by the people of a few Hindi-speaking States only, will go a long way in successfully giving to the programmes like Family Planning, an added fillip curtailing the monotony of incomprehension as also in realizing our desired goals of population control in India.

These will drive home the people living in the far-flung areas o the basic concept and idea of the programme, efficacy of various contraceptive devices and the need for controlled birth too.

61

Various misgivings including public misbeliefs that a child is a gift o God, which, if impeded, amounts to sin, may also be allayed considerably through such programmes.

Towards achieving this noble end, various Village Community Halls and such other institutions may be provided with Radio, TV and Video sets. This will ensure a regular get-together and freeexchange o creative views amongst both the sexes which will, in turn, stimulate adaptability and work, they all having the warmth of the much desired proximity to one another, as a panacaea against excessive sensuality, cardinal desire, and abnormal propensity towards early marriages and such other abuses.

The teachings of noted doctors, great leaders, philosophers, pundits and prophets including such other noted personalities on various aspects of marital relations may also be included in such programames to rouse public awareness and prevail upon the religiously orthodox minds.

Different social and voluntary organizations may also play a precursory role in raising the social status of woman, relaxing the so-called exercise of prudish, removing polygamy etc. by involving man and woman equally in various welfare and other economic, creative, reformative and rehabilitative activities through establishment of various Widow and Destitute Home, Weaving Centres and such other institutions, and thereby contribute liberally to the great task of national emancipation. 62

Also the government should remove all slums and arrange for some alternative off-season avocations and open up avenues for various agrobased industries in the rural areas for the agriculturists and labour-classes. Different rural development programmes like IRDP. NREP etc. need special thrust and sincere government effort not only for employment generation, poverty alleviation and raising peoples' economic status but also to keep them busy engaged in some lucrative jobs away from home and to prevent accordingly their enticement and lust for women entertainment and the like. Meanwhile, to quote from the Hindi file, "Mein Aaur Tum", which has to to say --- sex, simultaneously a mystic deity and virgin of heaven, is some sort of hunger, which cannot go unmet for so prolonged a period, the hollowness of which can, once unearthed only through timely and legal wedlocks, dillute all human fantasy. As we take rice to fill the belly and meet our hunger, so is the case with marriage also, which if checked injudiciously for unduly longer time, will not only cause late marriages leading to sex-starvation but also shall have no leg to stand by and thereby make the life of many a youngmen and the would-be parents miserable by way of various debilities, debauchery, late parenthood, delayed education of the children and so forth.

In fine, one believes that under a given situation like various socio-religious behaviours of our

63

people when changed, different restrictions liberally relaxed, a minimal liberty to exercise free will in terms of various interactions amongst both the sexes such as games and sports, as also of marriages to some extent encouraged and allowed, may reap well and stimulate increasing public response in cooperating with the government for successful achievement of the national goals towards curbing the population menace, and unless this is done the concept o marriage and population control will continue to remain as serious a problem as ever.

(Filed to newspapers by A. Islam sometime in late eighties)

o0o

www.ingramcontent.com/pod-product-compliance
Lightning Source LLC
La Vergne TN
LVHW050422160726
843469LV00041B/1188